Marguerite's Fountain

For Serena
with love,
in celebration
of all the dancing.
R.E.

For Jan
my dear friend
P.B.

Written by
Rachel Elliot

Illustrated by
Petra Brown

This edition published 2009 by Little Bee
an imprint of Meadowside Children's Books

First published in 2008
by Meadowside Children's Books
185 Fleet Street London EC4A 2HS
www.meadowsidebooks.com

Text © Rachel Elliot 2008
Illustrations © Petra Brown 2008
The rights of Rachel Elliot and
Petra Brown to be identified
as the author and illustrator of this work
have been asserted by them in accordance
with the Copyright, Designs
and Patents Act, 1988

A CIP catalogue record for this book
is available from the British Library
10 9 8 7 6 5 4 3 2 1
Printed in Malaysia

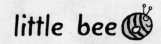

little bee

enjamin lived at the
bottom of the tallest steeple
in the cathedral yard. There was
a little gap in the sturdy stone.
It had been there for hundreds
and hundreds of years.

Marguerite
lived next to
the little fountain.
All day and all night
the sparkling drops
danced in the
fountain pool.

Every day Benjamin watched
Marguerite dancing around the fountain.
He longed to be friends with her
but Benjamin was shy and didn't dare.

So Marguerite danced alone.

Then, one day, someone
was dancing with Marguerite.
His name was Randolph.
His coat was dark and glossy
and his eyes were as
black as oil.

Randolph wanted to
have the little fountain
for his own.
"You are the most beautiful
dancer I have ever known,"
he told Marguerite.

Benjamin wanted to tell
Marguerite the truth.
But Randolph was big and strong.
Benjamin was small and scared.

"You have a lovely voice."
So Marguerite danced for
Randolph and sparkled for him.
But he was lying.

So he said nothing.

But one day,
Randolph stopped
telling Marguerite she
was a beautiful dancer.

"You're making me dizzy
with all that spinning!"
he shouted. Then he stopped
telling her that she had a lovely voice.

"Be quiet!" he shouted.
"I want to listen to the
sound of my fountain!"

"Your fountain?" gasped Marguerite.

Randolph twirled his thin moustache and laughed.

"It is my fountain now," he said. "You must find somewhere else to live. The sewer is empty, you can live there."

Benjamin watched Marguerite creep away from her little fountain.

Marguerite
no longer sparkled
and danced.
She curled up in the
old sewer alone.

"I am the King of the World!"
Randolph laughed, marching around the fountain.

"I wish I was strong
and brave,"
sighed Benjamin.

Then he had
an idea.

Benjamin
crept into the
deepest drain.

He ran through the dripping,
smelly pipes. It was dark and scary.

There were loud,
gurgling noises
all around him.

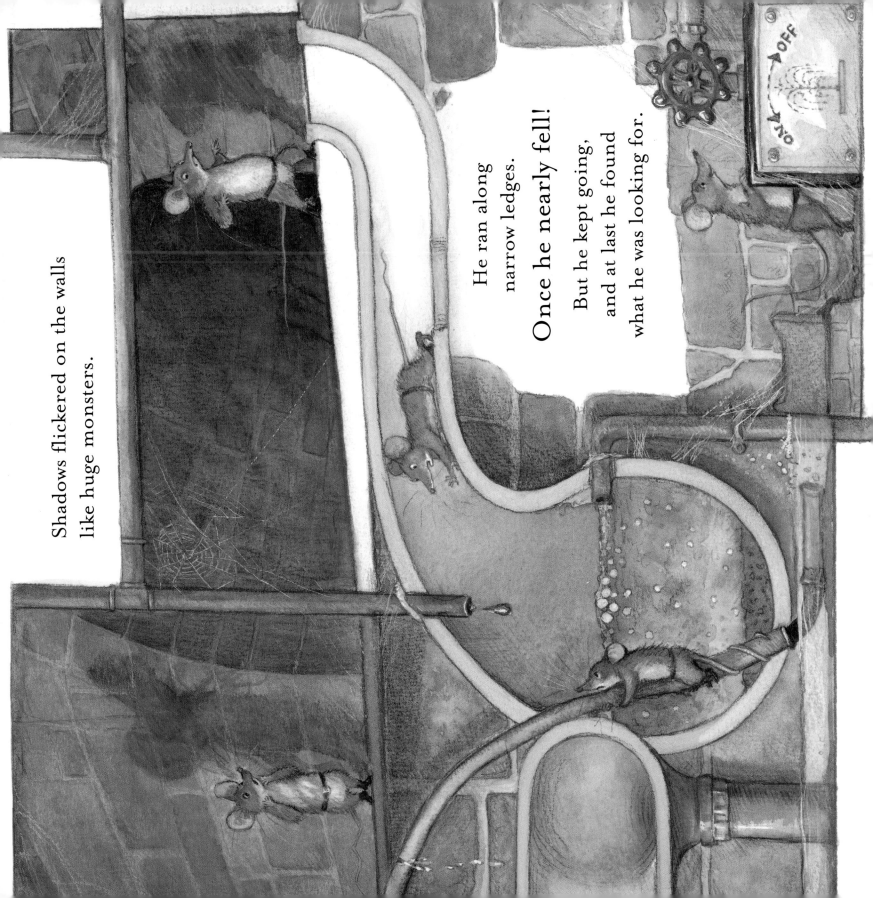

Shadows flickered on the walls like huge monsters.

He ran along narrow ledges.

Once he nearly fell!

But he kept going, and at last he found what he was looking for.

Next morning,
the little fountain was silent and still.
"Work!" shouted Randolph.

Nothing happened.

"What is wrong with my fountain?"
Randolph roared.

Benjamin was standing by the drain.
"The fountain is missing Marguerite," he said.
"You have to bring her back."

Randolph ran to the sewer and dragged poor
Marguerite out. Her coat was muddy
and her whiskers were crumpled.

Randolph waited.

But the fountain was
still and silent just like before.
"You lied to me!"
Randolph shouted at Benjamin.
Benjamin's paws were shaking,
but he hid them behind
his back.

"The fountain
is unhappy because
Marguerite is unhappy,"
he told Randolph.
"You have to be kind
to her."

He straightened her whiskers. He told her that she was beautiful. He gave her good things to eat.

Randolph growled and grumbled, but he wanted the fountain to work more than anything. So he helped Marguerite clean her coat.

But Marguerite did not smile or sing or dance.
And the little fountain was silent and still.

"You lied to me!" Randolph shouted again.

Benjamin was so frightened his little tail

was shaking.

Marguerite looked at Benjamin.
She could not bear to see
Randolph scare him.

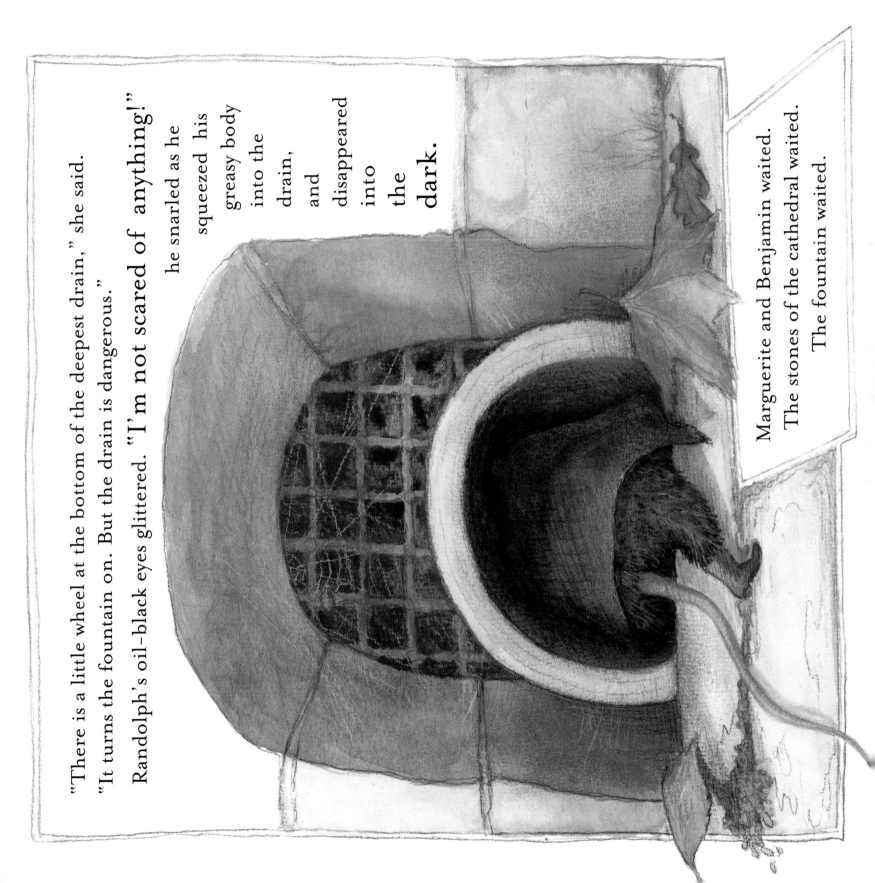

"There is a little wheel at the bottom of the deepest drain," she said.

"It turns the fountain on. But the drain is dangerous."

Randolph's oil-black eyes glittered. "I'm not scared of anything!"

he snarled as he squeezed his greasy body into the drain, and disappeared into the **dark.**

Marguerite and Benjamin waited.
The stones of the cathedral waited.
The fountain waited.

Then there was
a movement in the drain.
Randolph slid out onto
the ground. He was dirty
and muddy and smelly,
and he was shaking
all over.

"Monsters!" he said.
"Gurgling, dripping monsters!"
He squirmed on the ground.
His eyes flickered
from side to side.

"I can do this," Benjamin whispered. He took a long deep breath, and disappeared into the drain.

Marguerite and Randolph waited. The stones of the cathedral waited. The fountain waited.

At last, Benjamin stepped out of the drain. He was dirty and muddy and smelly, but his bright eyes were full of fire.

"You are a coward!" he said.

"Your heart is as stony as the cathedral and as tiny as a single drop of water!"

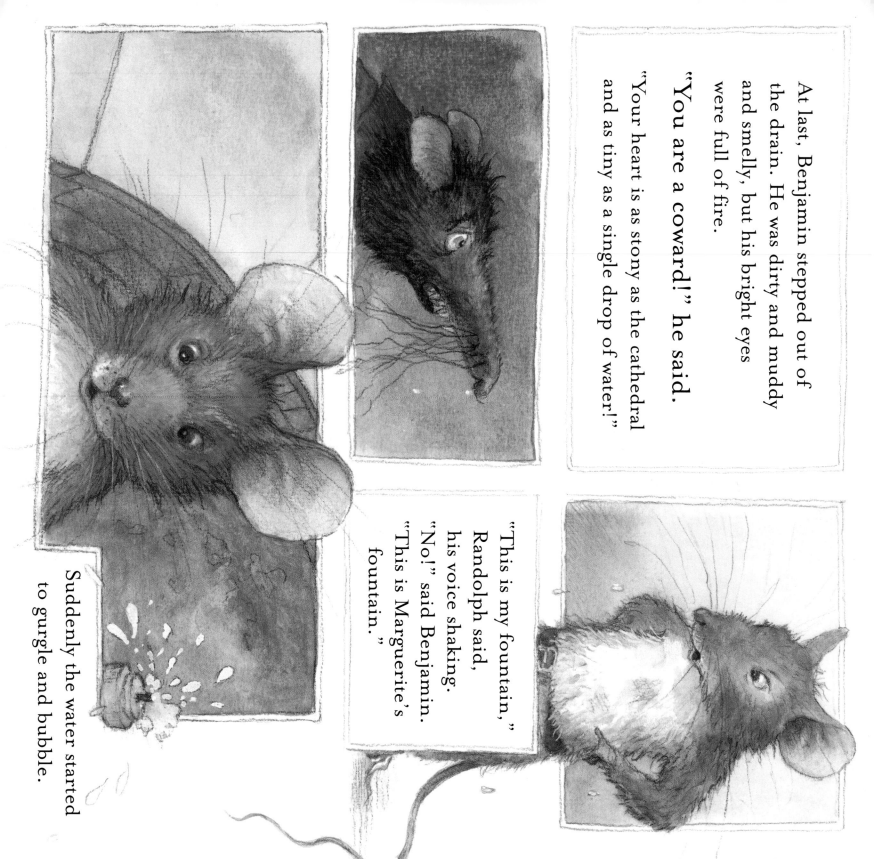

Suddenly the water started to gurgle and bubble.

"This is my fountain," Randolph said, his voice shaking.
"No!" said Benjamin.
"This is Marguerite's fountain."

"Leave now,"
Benjamin said.
"Leave the fountain,
and leave the cathedral
yard, and leave
Marguerite alone!"

Randolph's moustache drooped. He looked
at the fountain, at Benjamin, then at Marguerite.

"I don't care about your silly fountain anyway,"
he muttered and slowly slithered away
into the shadows.

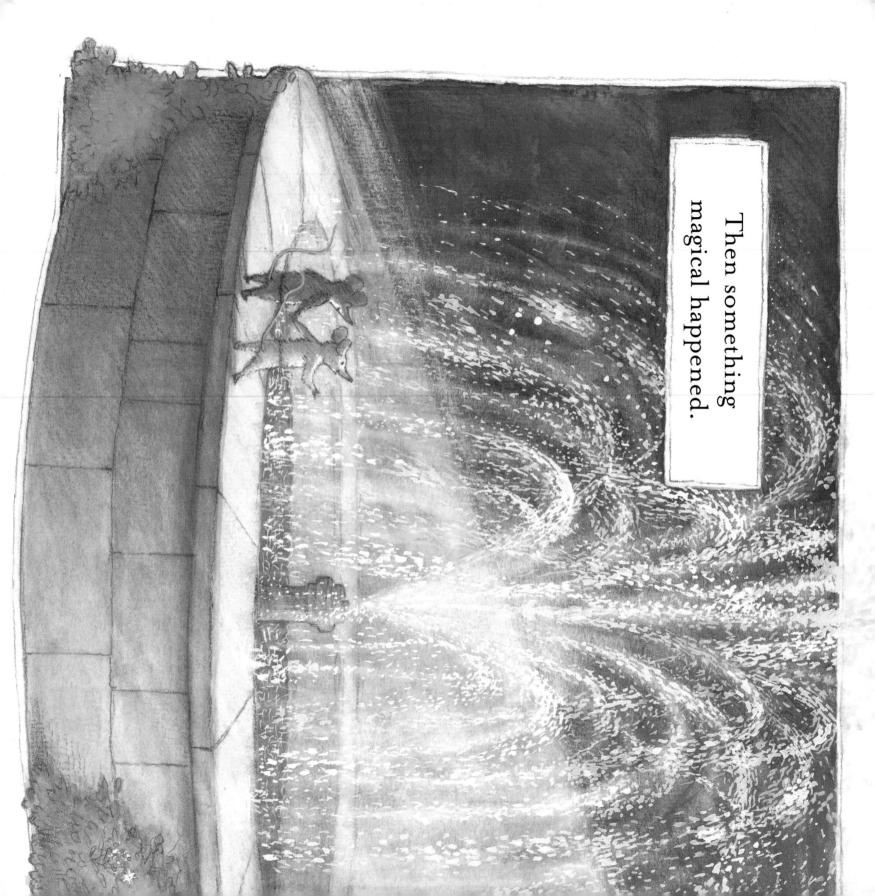

Then something magical happened.

The fountain
burst into life!
The water foamed
and frothed and flew
into the air,
higher and higher,
until it was as high as
the highest steeple
in the cathedral yard!

Now everything is
just as before.

Almost everything.

Marguerite still dances around the fountain...

...But now
Benjamin dances with her.